The Ghost in the Lagoon

The Ghost
in the Lagoon

by Natalie Savage Carlson

illustrations by Andrew Glass

Lothrop, Lee & Shepard Books   New York

For Sara Margaret Rondolino,
the prettiest baby I have ever seen

Library of Congress Cataloging in Publication Data. Carlson, Natalie Savage. The ghost in the lagoon. Summary: Timmy finds a way to outwit the pirate's ghost that stands guard over a buried treasure. [1. Ghosts—Fiction. 2. Buried treasure— Fiction] I. Glass, Andrew, ill. II. Title. PZ7.C2167Gh 1984   [Fic]   83-25114 ISBN 0-688-03794-1   ISBN 0-688-03795-X (lib. bdg.)

Contents

1

A Catfish Night

Way down South, Timmy Hawkins lived with his parents in a tumbledown shack on a poor piece of land. Their cornfield was guarded by a scarecrow whose clothes were tattered. A shapeless hat flopped over his face, as if the scarecrow did not wish to be seen.

One year, the corn crop was so poor that there was little food on the Hawkins' table.

The father said, "I will go fishing in the lagoon out yonder tonight. There should be plenty of catfish in that muddy water."

"Oh, no!" cried his wife. "They say it is haunted. No one will go there at night. Even hunting dogs chasing a possum turn back if the possum makes a run for the lagoon."

"But night's when catfish bite best," said the father, "and it's when the possum come out of their hidey-holes. That's what they say."

"I'll go with you, Pa," said Timmy, "if you'll let me do some of the fishing."

So that night, they set out for the lagoon.

The father carried the fishing pole and the boy
the lantern. They went *whish, whish* through
the tall weeds and stunted oaks to the water's
edge. The lantern's light showed crooked shadows creeping through the trees as if spying on
them. Hanging moss brushed their faces like
ghostly fingers.

They sat down on a low mound at the edge of the lagoon. The father baited the hook.

"You can throw the line and hold the pole," he said to Timmy.

Whish! The boy flung the line into the dark water.

There was a sharp tug on the line, and they heard a louder *WHISH* like the slash of a knife.

The line broke in two, and Timmy fell backward.
A loon's mocking laugh came from a nearby
clump of cattails. Or was it a loon?

"Must have been a granddaddy catfish to
break that line," said the father. "I'll make a
stronger one, and we'll try again tomorrow
night. Sure would like you to catch a catfish.
They can be mighty good!"

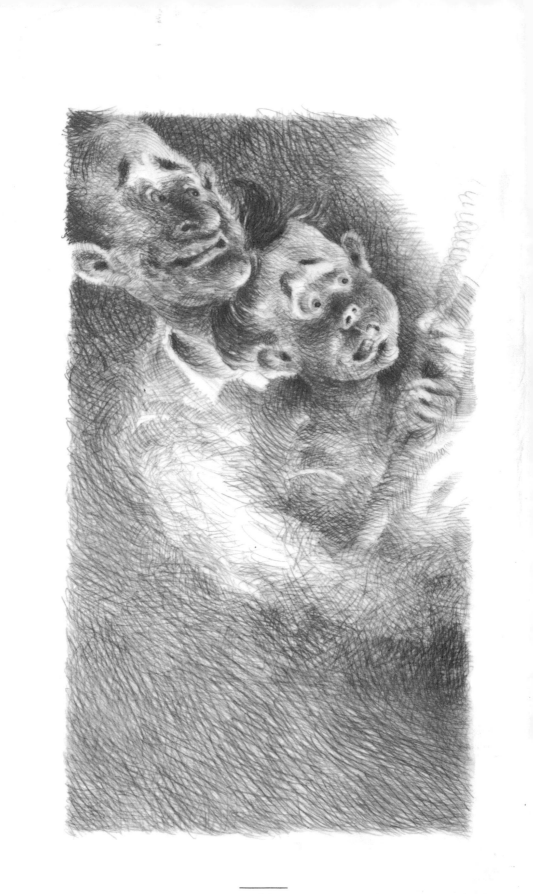

Surprise!

So they set forth the next night. Timmy tossed out the line with a *whish*. Something grabbed the line and tugged so hard that Timmy and the pole were dragged into the water. His father tried to pull him back on the bank. But Timmy kept slipping into the weeds and mud at the water's edge.

"Something's got hold of me," he gasped. "Something's trying to drown me."

But at last his father was able to get him back on dry land. "Must have been an alligator pulling on that line," he told Timmy. "I'll make a new pole, and best I do the fishing tomorrow night."

They hurried home, *whish, whish, whish,* through the weeds so Timmy could change into dry clothes.

The father cut a new fishing pole the next morning. Then he made an even stronger line.

That night he said to the boy, "If an alligator gets the hook tonight, I'll let go of the pole fast."

They went *whish, whish* through the weeds.

The shadows in the oaks moved closer and closer to them. The hanging moss clawed at their faces. But they didn't see an alligator on the bank, and so they sat down on the mound. The father tossed the line, *whish*, into the water.

Suddenly an eerie form appeared.

It wasn't an alligator. It was a man in a plumed hat, with a pistol in his sash.

"Haven't I given you enough warning to stay away from here?" he demanded in a hollow voice.

Whish! He waved a cutlass at them. "Next time, I'll cut you into bait for your hook."

"It's a pirate's ghost!" cried Timmy.

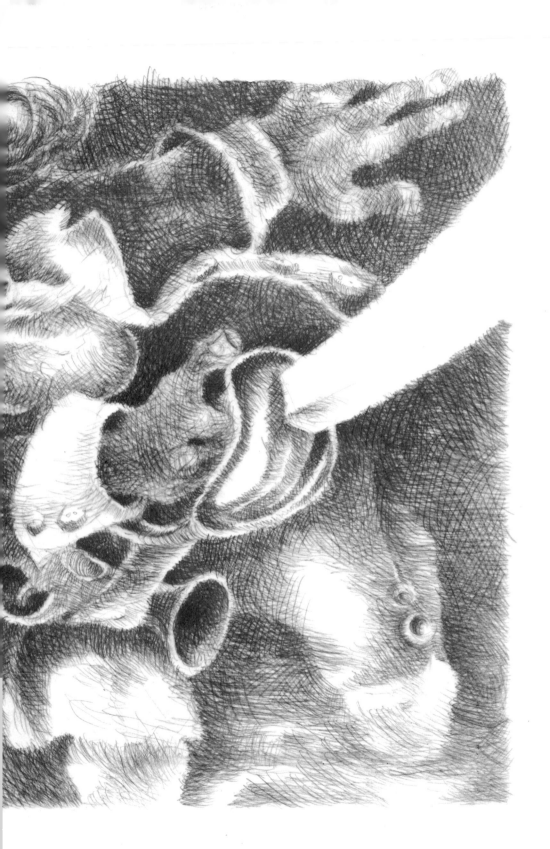

19

They jumped up and ran, *bump, bump* into trees and through the weeds, *whish, whish, whisher.*

The father told his wife, "The lagoon is haunted by a pirate's ghost. That's why neither man nor dog dare go there at night. First the ghost cut Timmy's line. Then he tried to drown him."

3

Treasure Hunt

Timmy said, "He must be guarding treasure buried in the mound. That's why he wants to keep us away."

The father said, "If only *he* would go away, we could dig up the treasure. We certainly need it."

Timmy said, "Let's go there during the day and dig for it. Ghosts are only about at night. That's what they say."

The next day, his father took the shovel, and Timmy went with him to take turns with the digging. The oaks didn't look so scary in the daylight. The moss hung gray and still.

The father pushed the shovel into the mound. *Stomp, whish, CRACK!* The handle broke off and flew at Timmy's head.

"I think the ghost did it, even if we can't see him," said the boy, rubbing the bump on his head.

His father said, "Best we give up digging and fishing. Better to go hungry than have you get a cracked head or be drowned!"

So the family had less and less to eat. Timmy grew angrier and angrier with the ghost.

On Halloween, the boy dressed as a ghost himself because an old sheet was the only costume he had. Even the moon looked haunted as he set out for the little town at the crossroads, hoping to fill his sack with the tasty treats his family couldn't buy.

As he went through the corn stubbles, he was suddenly startled at sight of the scarecrow. In the moonlight, the scarecrow looked like a ghost too.

That scarecrow gave Timmy an idea. But did he dare? As he looked up at the spooky Halloween moon, he thought, "This is the night to try it."

Timmy's Plan

Timmy pulled off the old sheet he was wearing and draped it over the scarecrow and himself.

"You will make me into a bigger ghost," he said. "And I need to be a great big one for this."

Timmy headed for the lagoon, holding the ghostly scarecrow high in the moonlight. He carried it, *whish, whish,* through the weeds.

The bare oak branches snatched at the sheet as if they were trying to keep Timmy from the

lagoon. The hanging moss pulled at the boy.

He wanted to run back home, like the hunting dogs. They could scent danger, as well as possums. But he already had come this far. Timmy told himself, "I must carry out my plan!"

When he reached the bank, he held the scare-crow higher.

"Oo-oo-oo!" Timmy moaned. "I've come to see you."

At once, the pirate's ghost appeared.
"Who are you, and why have you come here?"
he demanded. "The treasure is mine."

Timmy raised the scarecrow higher than the pirate's plumed hat.

"I am the ghost of one of your victims," replied the boy in a voice muffled by the sheet. "I'm not after the treasure. I have come for *you.*

They've sent me to bring you to the fires below
for your wicked deeds."

"No, no!" cried the frightened pirate. "I won't go with you."

He disappeared in the night.

Timmy hurried home.

When his father heard of his daring deed, he first scolded him. Then he praised Timmy for frightening the pirate's ghost.

Timmy said, "He seemed so scared, I don't think he will come back soon."

5

Another Try

So the next day, they went to the mound with a new shovel. The father began to dig, *stomp, whish, stomp, whish.* Timmy held his breath. Had the pirate's ghost really been frightened enough to stay away? What would happen if he came back? He would surely cut them into bait.

But the shovel didn't break. Soon it scraped against something hard. *Scrunch, scrunch.* A few more digs, and there was a small rusted chest.

They carried the chest back to their tumbledown shack, bowed under by its weight. There, they pried it open. As they had hoped, the chest was filled with gold coins.

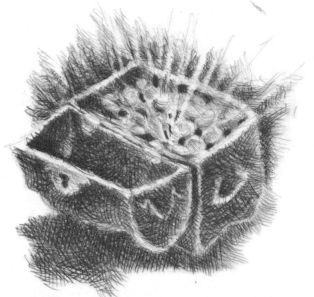

"These are better than catfish," said the father.

He used the gold to build a nice house on a better piece of land. From then on, there was plenty of food on the table. And the scarecrow always had good clothes.

The pirate's ghost never returned to the lagoon. But sometimes it is seen in other places way down South.

That's what they say.